DISNEY's TARZAN ®

Swing Time

**Cover illustrated by
Judith Clarke and Lori Tyminski,
painted by Andrea and John Alvin.**

Kala, a gorilla,
hears a strange sound
as she walks
through the jungle. It sounds like
a baby crying. She follows the noise.
Soon she is standing in front of a tree house.
She hears the baby cry again.

Kala finds the baby underneath a blanket inside the tree house.

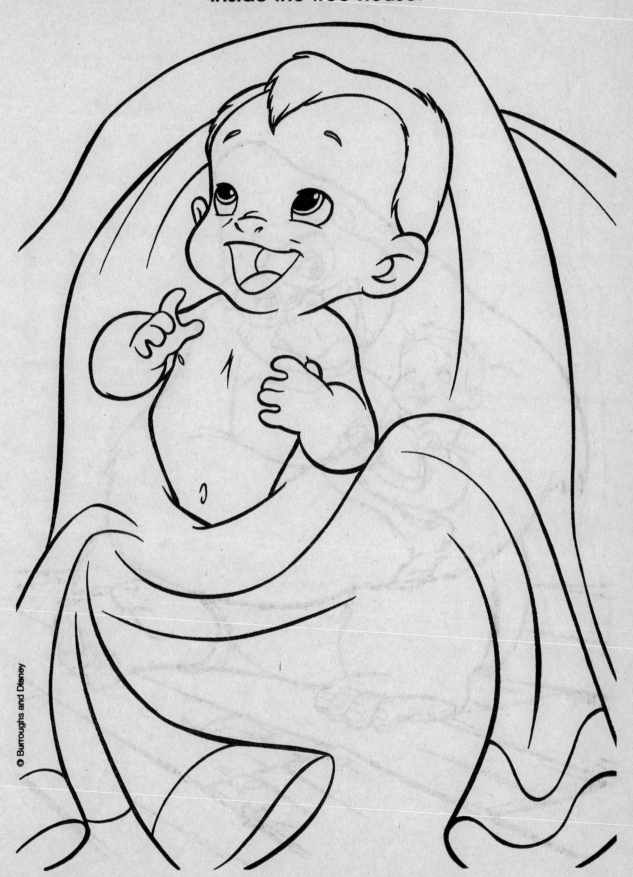

They like each other right away.

There is someone else in the tree house!

LEOPARD MATCH
Which picture of Sabor matches the outline at the top of the page?

A

B

C

D

Sabor pounces at Kala and the baby.

Kala and the baby escape safely.

Terk, a young ape, holds the human baby.

**"I'm going to be his mother now,"
says Kala.**

**"I'm going to be his mother now,"
says Kala.**

Kerchak, the gorilla leader, is afraid the baby will bring danger to his family.

THE NAME GAME
What does Kala name the baby? To find out, write the first letter of the name of each picture on the lines below.

$\overline{}$ 1 $\overline{}$ 2 $\overline{}$ 3 $\overline{}$ 4 $\overline{}$ 5 $\overline{}$ 6

Answers: tent, ape, rainbow, zebra, apple, nest: TARZAN

Tarzan tries to be just like the other gorillas,
but they don't always want the
"hairless wonder" hanging around.
One day Tarzan accidentally causes
an elephant stampede.
Kerchak is very angry and says
Tarzan will never fit in with
the gorilla family.

Maybe mud will help him look more like a gorilla.

"Why am I so different?"

HAND TO HAND
Does your hand look like Kala's?
To find out, place your hand on the next page
and use a pen or pencil to trace it.
What is different between her hand and yours?

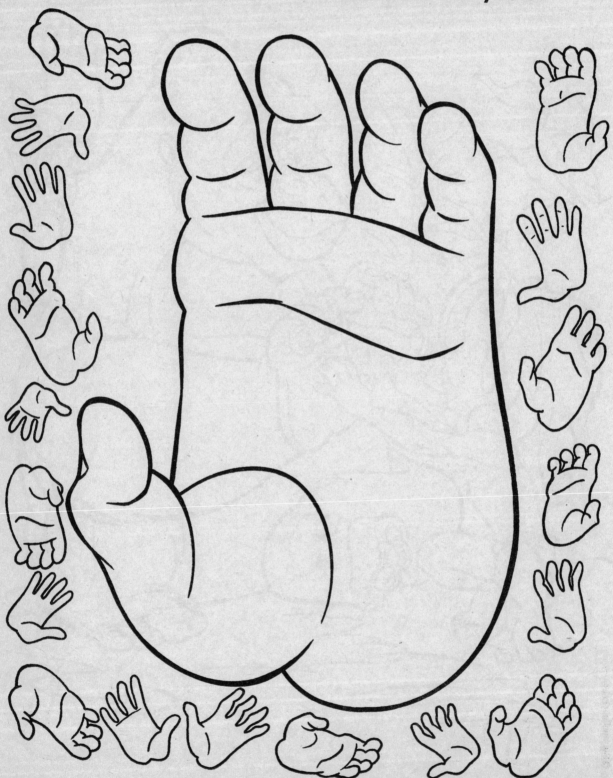

Trace your hand here.

Kala tells Tarzan that inside they are the same. They each have a heart.

Tarzan grows up. He has learned to dive . . .

. . . and to swing through the trees.

SWING TIME
Which vine is Tarzan holding?

A   B   C   D

Answer: B

The apes cheer for Tarzan when he
defeats their enemy, Sabor.

Soon the gorillas hear
a loud BLAM!
They go off to hide.
But Tarzan decides to
investigate. He hides in a tree
watching three strange creatures.
There are humans in the jungle!

Professor Porter has come to study gorillas.

Clayton is the guide for the expedition.

Jane and her father are very excited
when they find gorilla nests.

**Before long, Jane comes across
a baby baboon.**

**He wants the picture
Jane has drawn of him.**

ANIMAL ART
Draw a picture of your favorite jungle animal in Jane's sketchbook.

Soon hundreds of baboons are chasing Jane.

MAKE A PAIR
Jane loses a boot in the chase. Which boot matches the one at the top of the page?

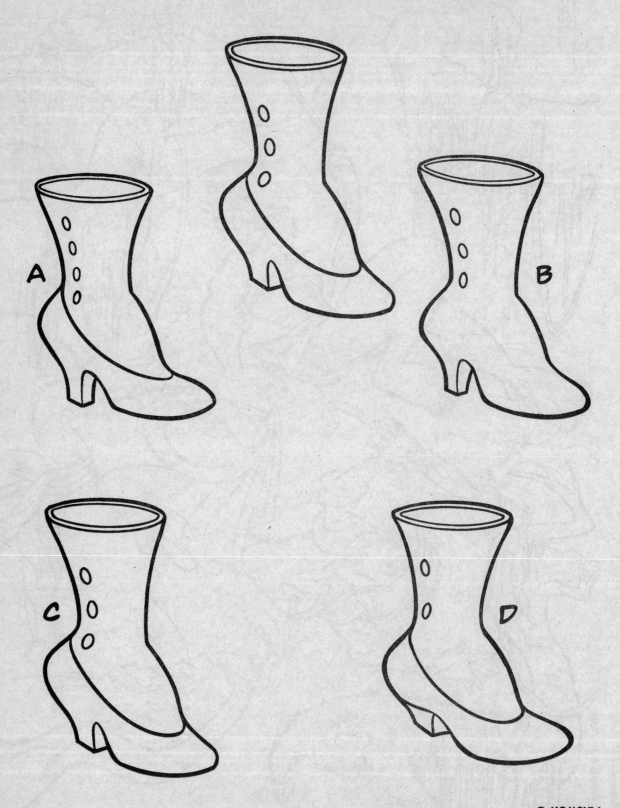

When Tarzan examines Jane's foot, she starts to giggle.

Their hands are similar.

And they each have a heart!

"I'm Jane."

"Tarzan."

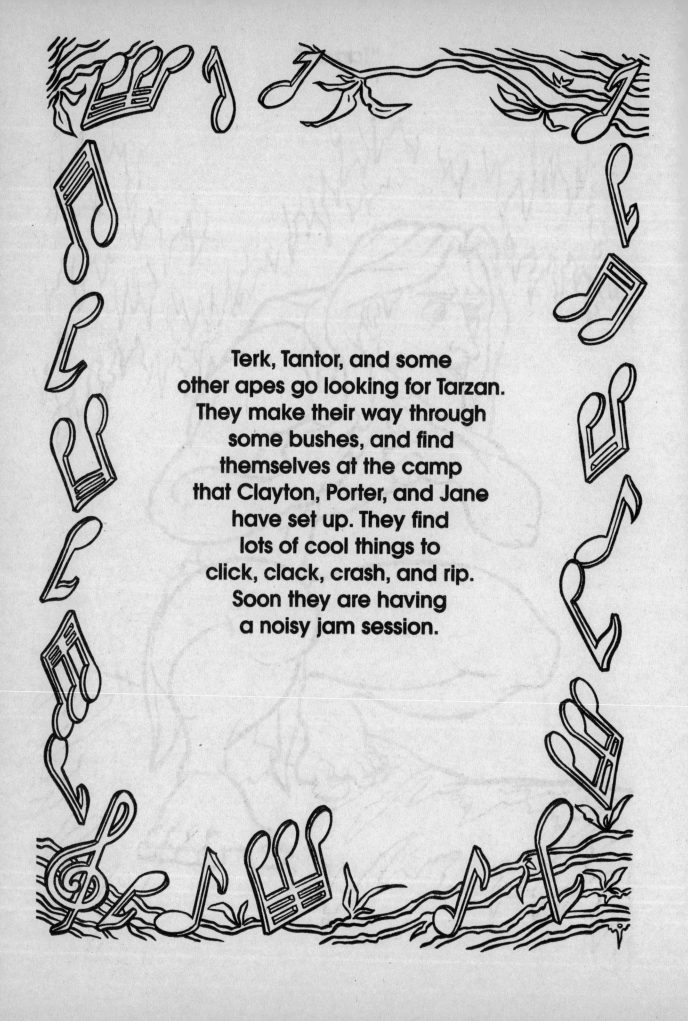

Terk, Tantor, and some
other apes go looking for Tarzan.
They make their way through
some bushes, and find
themselves at the camp
that Clayton, Porter, and Jane
have set up. They find
lots of cool things to
click, clack, crash, and rip.
Soon they are having
a noisy jam session.

"Ding! I love that part."

Tantor is a good "trumpet" player.

Forks and spoons make great sounds.

JAMMIN' IN THE JUNGLE
You can make your own instruments at home and start a jungle band!

MONKEY MUSIC
You will need:

coffee tin or
plastic container

dried beans

1. Pour a handful of dried beans into a container.
2. Put the top securely on the container.
3. Start shaking it and make some music!

JUNGLE DRUM
You will need:

coffee tin
with plastic cover

wooden mixing spoon

1. Put the plastic top on a clean, empty coffee tin.
2. Use wooden mixing spoon to bang your drum!

HIPPO HARMONICA
You will need:

comb   wax paper   rubber band

1. Cut the wax paper to the size of the length of the comb.
2. Place the paper against one side of the comb and secure it in place with the rubber band.
3. Hold the paper side against your mouth and hum a tune!

BABOON BANJO
You will need:

empty rectangular tissue box   4 rubber bands

1. Place the rubber bands around the box so they stretch across the opening.
2. Strum the banjo and sing along!

Jane tells the others about meeting Tarzan.

Jane shows her father how Tarzan moves.

Tarzan comes back and surprises everyone.

JUNGLE FRIENDS

Look up, down, across, back, and diagonally
to find the names in the puzzle.

JANE   KALA   TANTOR   TARZAN   TERK   PORTER

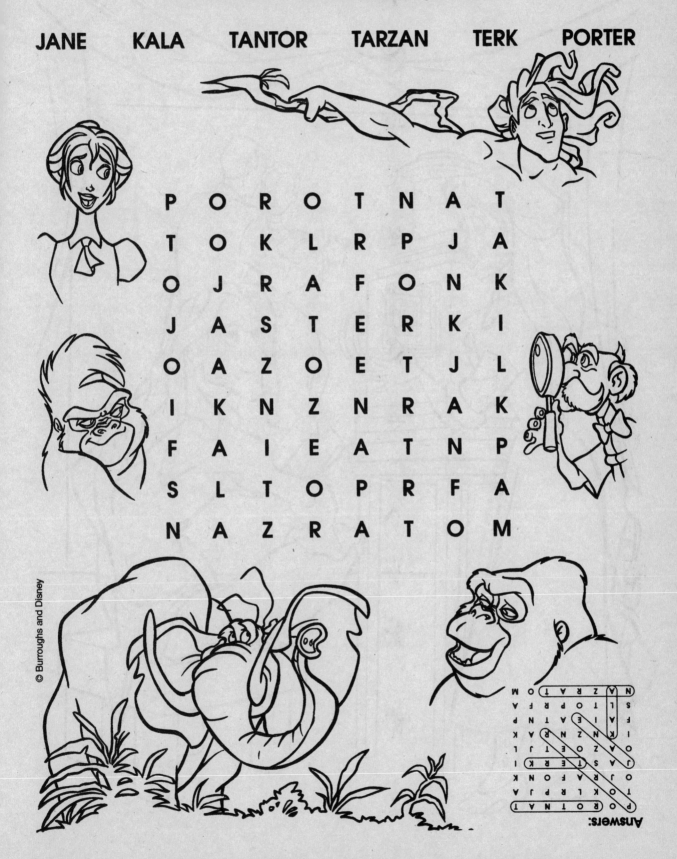

P O R O T N A T
T O K L R P J A
O J R A F O N K
J A S T E R K I
O A Z O E T J L
I K N Z N R A K
F A I E A T N P
S L T O P R F A
N A Z R A T O M

Jane shows Tarzan slides to teach him about the human world.

Tarzan shows Jane part of his world, high up in the trees.

READY, SET, COUNT!
How many birds can you count?

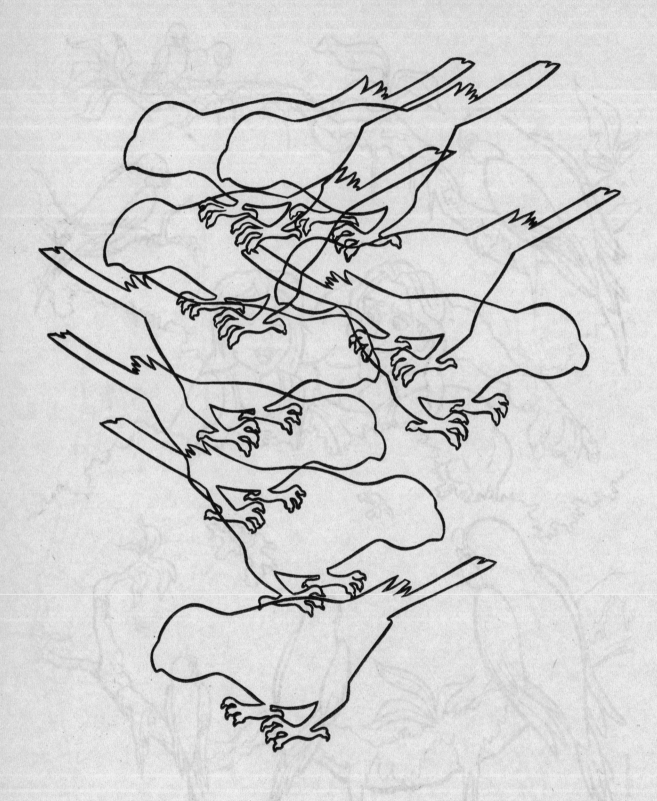

Jane begins to feel at home in the jungle.

Clayton wants to find the gorillas.

FLOWER POWER
Draw flowers on the stems so Tarzan will have a nice bouquet to give to Jane.

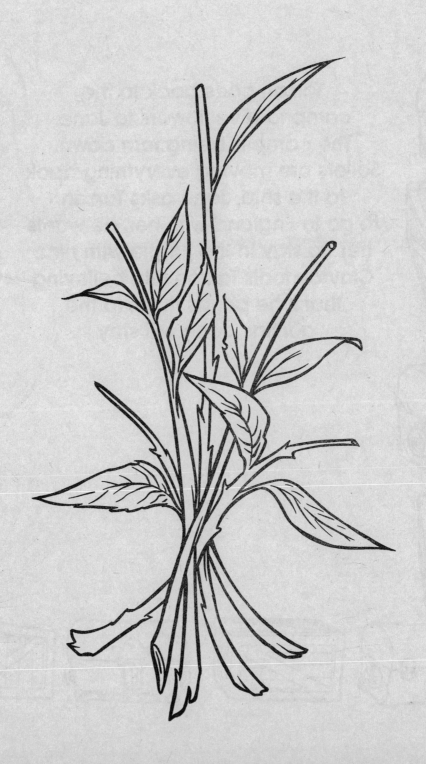

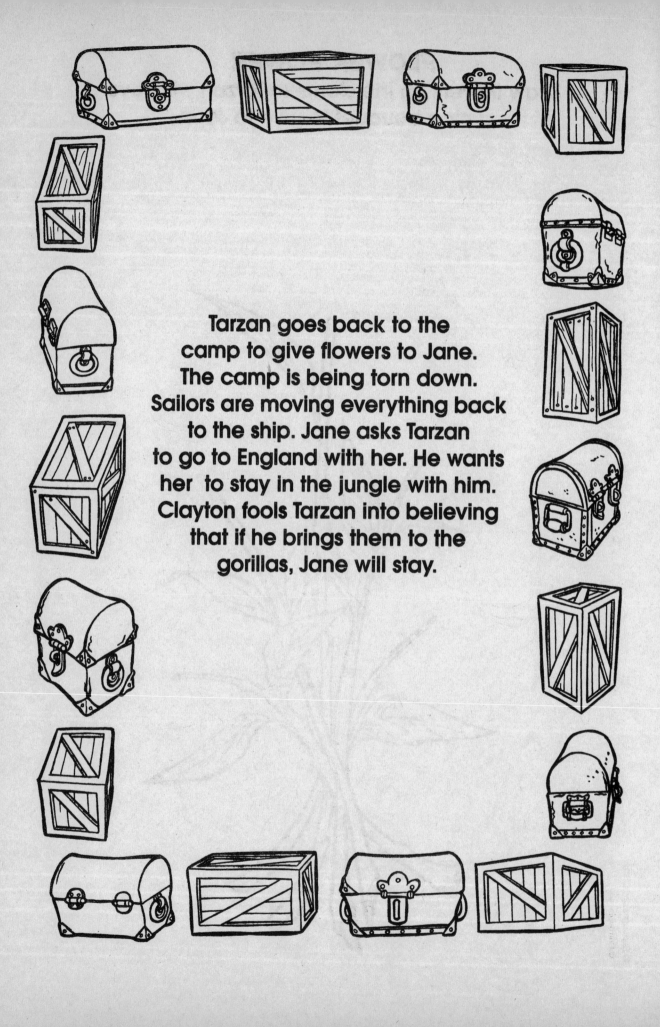

Tarzan goes back to the
camp to give flowers to Jane.
The camp is being torn down.
Sailors are moving everything back
to the ship. Jane asks Tarzan
to go to England with her. He wants
her to stay in the jungle with him.
Clayton fools Tarzan into believing
that if he brings them to the
gorillas, Jane will stay.

Tarzan asks for a favor.

Terk and Tantor agree to disguise themselves
so that Kerchak will run after them.

Now Tarzan can bring the humans to the gorillas.

MAKE A PORTER PUPPET

You can make your own Porter puppet.
First color Porter's head and body. Then ask an adult to
cut them out along the dotted lines.
Glue the head and body to a paper bag (see drawing).
Place your hand in the bag and you're ready to go
exploring with the professor!

Jane can't believe her eyes!

Tarzan tells the apes not to be afraid.

Gorillas come out of the trees.

Porter meets
the gorillas.

HAT MATCH
Which two hats are exactly alike?

A

B

C

D

E

Answers: B and E

Clayton does not like it when one
of the gorillas grabs his rifle.

Jane loves the cute babies.

Uh-oh! Here comes Kerchak!

Kerchak sees Clayton
arguing with one of the gorillas.
He charges at Clayton. Tarzan grabs
Kerchak and holds him back. Tarzan yells
for the humans to leave. When the
humans are gone, Kerchak tells Tarzan
that he betrayed them all by putting
his gorilla family in danger.

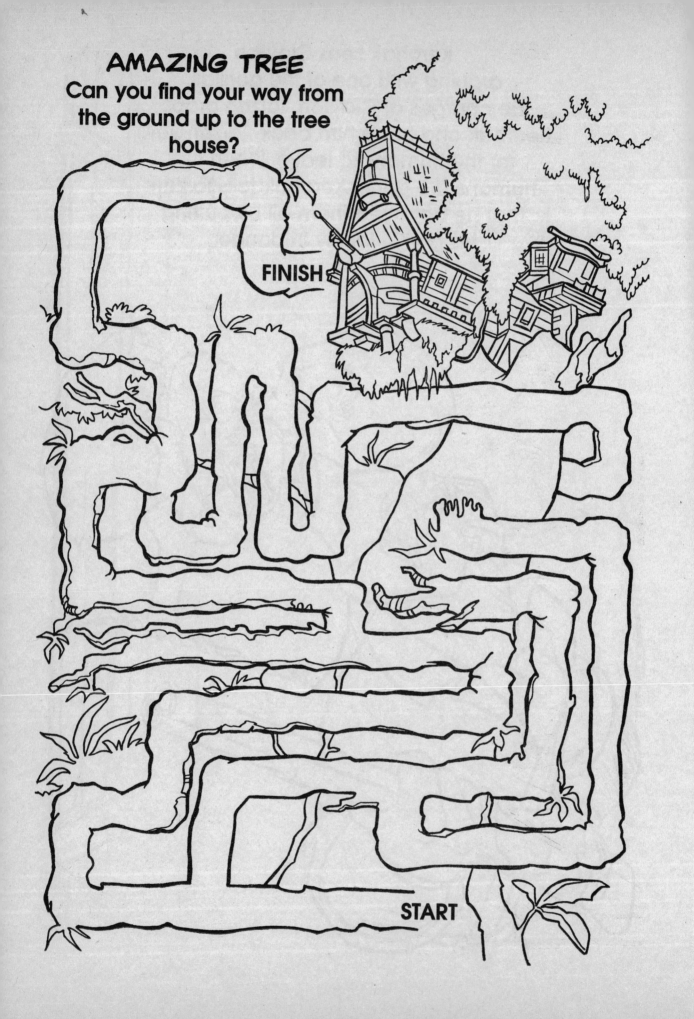

Later, Kala takes Tarzan to the tree house where she found him.

Tarzan goes over to the cradle.

Then he finds a picture of himself with his parents.

"No matter where I go,
you will always be my mother."

Tarzan joins Jane and Porter.

Once aboard the ship,
Jane, Porter, and Tarzan are taken prisoners.
Clayton tells them his evil plan.
He is going to capture the gorillas and
sell them! Tarzan feels responsible that his
family is in danger. He lets out a yell so
loud that it is heard by Terk and
Tantor, who are near the shore.

Terk and Tantor come to Tarzan's rescue.

Tarzan goes back to save his family.

Tarzan's friends help him rescue the gorillas.

Kala and the others are freed from their cages.

Jane decides to stay in the jungle with Tarzan.

Tarzan is the new leader of the apes!